BEAR IN A SQUARE

Written by Stella Blackstone
Illustrated by Debbie Harter

Barefoot Books
Celebrating Art and Story

www.barefootbooks.com

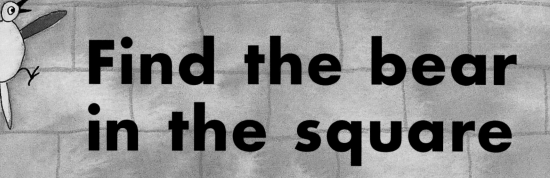

Find the bear
in the square

Find the hearts in the queen's hair

Find the circles in the pool

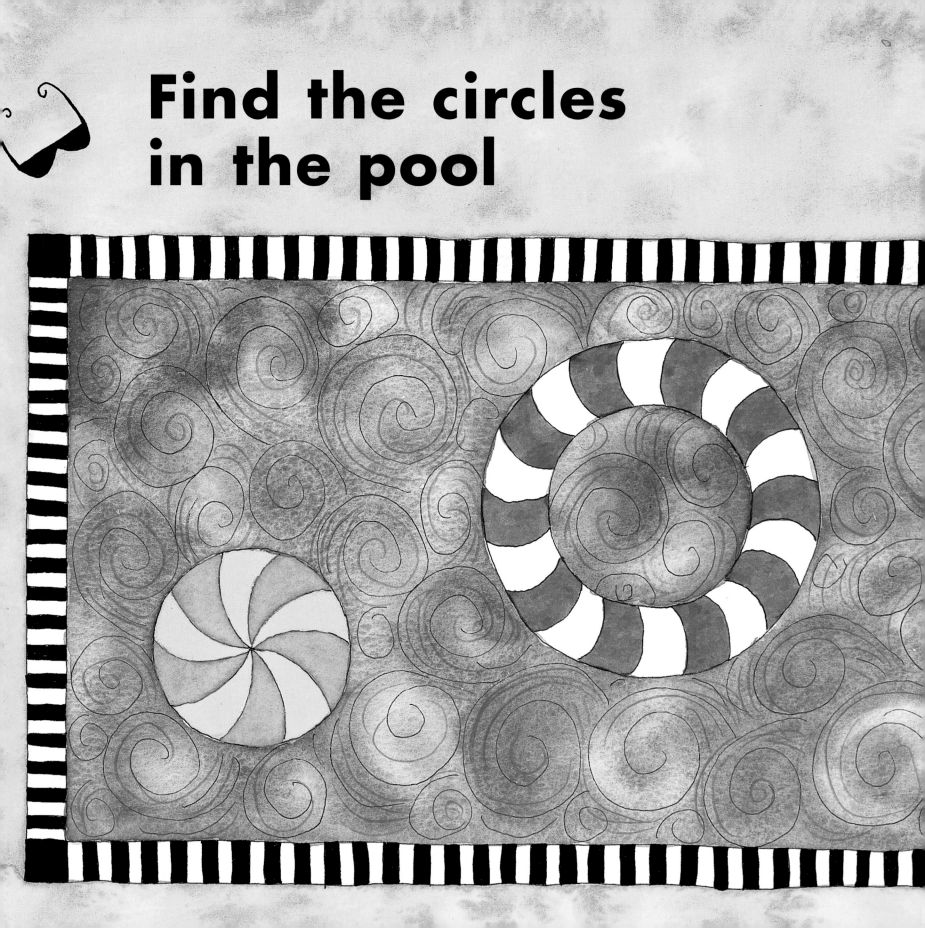

Find the rectangles
in the school

Find the moons in the cave

Find the triangles on the wave

Find the diamonds on the crown

Find the zigzags around the clown

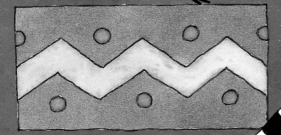

Find the ovals
in the park

Find the stars
in the dark

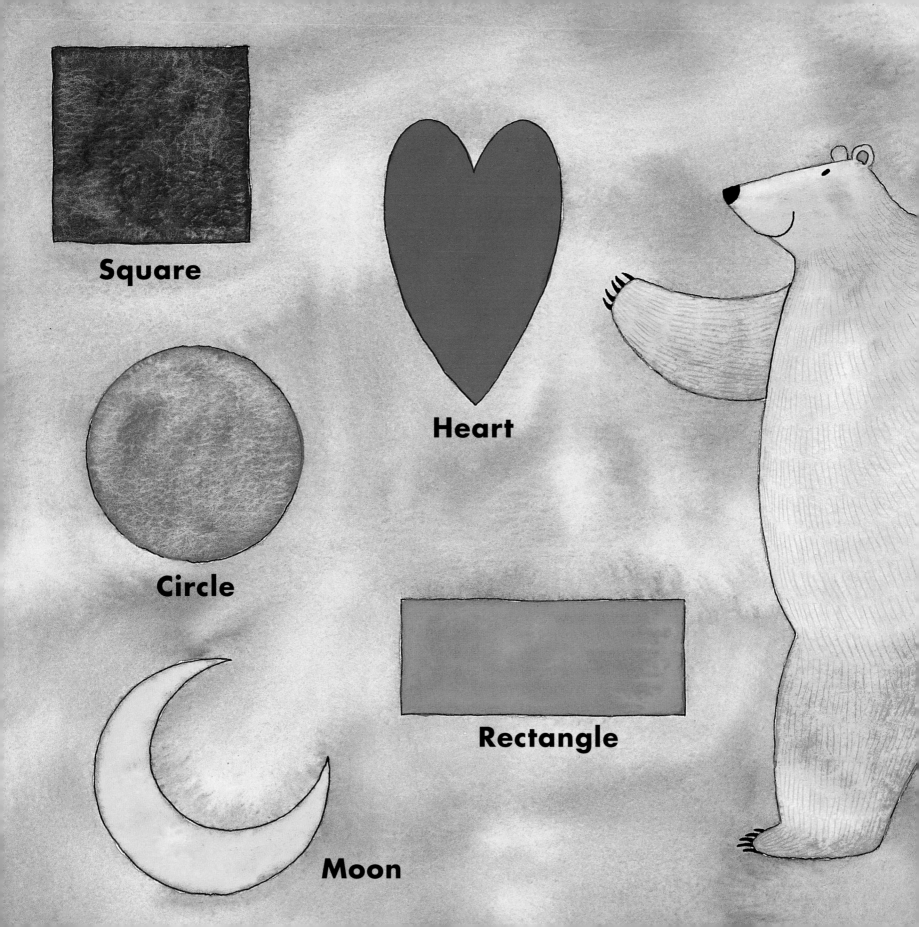

Square

Heart

Circle

Rectangle

Moon

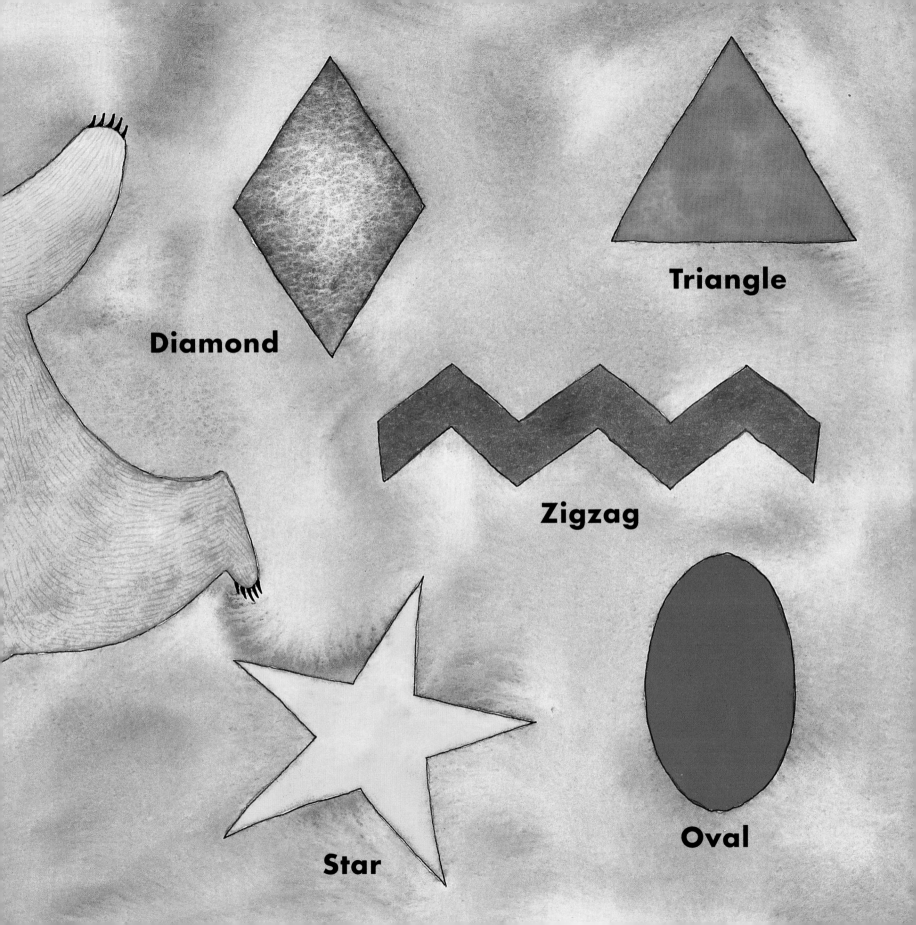

Diamond

Triangle

Zigzag

Star

Oval

Barefoot Books
3 Bow Street
Third Floor
Cambridge
MA 02138

First published in the United States of America in 1998 by Barefoot Books, Inc.
This paperback edition printed in 2002.

This book is printed on 100% acid-free paper

Graphic design by Jennie Hoare, England
Printed and bound in Singapore by Tien Wah Press (Pte) Ltd.

3 5 7 9 8 6 4 2

U.S. Cataloging-in-Publication Data / Library of Congress Standards

Blackstone, Stella.
    Bear in a square / written by Stella Blackstone ;
illustrated by Debbie Harter.
[32]p. : col. ill. ;   cm.
Summary: With a big friendly bear as a guide, you
can find shapes hidden on each page. With vibrant
artwork and rhyming text, children can recognize and
count squares, circles, triangles, zig-zags and stars.
ISBN 1-84148-120-3 (pbk.)
1. Shape. 2. Bears — Fiction. 3. Stories in rhyme.
I. Harter, Debbie, ill. II. Title.
[E]--dc21   1998   AC   CIP